Marlowe's Mum and the Tree House

First published in 2004 by
Franklin Watts
96 Leonard Street
London
EC2A 4XD

Franklin Watts Australia
45–51 Huntley Street
Alexandria
NSW 2015

A CIP catalogue record for this book is available from the British Library.

ISBN 0 7496 5870 3 (hbk)
ISBN 0 7496 5874 6 (pbk)

Series Editor: Jackie Hamley
Series Advisor: Dr Barrie Wade
Cover Design: Jason Anscomb
Design: Peter Scoulding

Printed in Hong Kong / China

For James and Nathaniel – K.L.

Marlowe's Mum and the Tree House

by Karina Law and Ross Collins

W
FRANKLIN WATTS
LONDON•SYDNEY

“Right! That’s it!” said Marlowe’s mum. “I’m getting out of here!”

"Where are you going?" asked Marlowe. Mum sounded cross.

"To the tree house. Maybe I'll get some peace up there," she said.

“But it’s teatime!” said Marlowe.

“Tell your dad,” replied Mum.

“I’ve had enough.”

“Dad,” said Marlowe,

“Mum’s left home.”

"Yes, Marlowe.
In a minute," said Dad.

"DAD," said Marlowe, a little louder. "MUM'S LEFT HOME!"

"LEFT HOME?" said Dad. "What do you mean, *left home*?"

"She's gone to my tree house," said Marlowe. Dad looked worried. "Perhaps she's not well," he said.

Dad called Doctor Frost.

“She’s a bit under the weather,” reported Doctor Frost. “Leave her for a day or two and I’m sure she’ll be as right as rain.”

Mrs Jones, from next door, popped round for a chat. Mum didn't seem to want to chat.

Dad left a tray of tea and cakes for Mum. But Mum didn't come down.

Mum was still up in the tree house at bedtime. Dad had to do *everything*.

Mum was still up in the tree house the next morning. But the tray had gone and there was a note.

Thank you for
the tea and cakes.
I like it up here.
Please bring me:
1. a hammer
2. nails
3. a saw
4. a spanner
5. some bolts
thank you very much.
Love Mum
x

“Nails?” said Dad with surprise.

“A hammer?” said Marlowe.

Marlowe and Dad fetched the things Mum wanted.

They left them at the foot of the ladder. “Perhaps Mum’s going to fix the leak in the roof of the tree house,” suggested Dad.

Everyone
missed Mum.

The next day, Mum was still in the tree house. There was a new note.

There were some very strange noises coming from the tree house.

Marlowe and Dad fetched the things Mum wanted and left them at the foot of the ladder.

"Perhaps Mum wants to do some cleaning," said Marlowe.

"On wheels?" asked Dad, shaking his head.

Mum stayed up in the tree house for three whole days. On the fourth day, at teatime, Mum came home.

Everyone was so pleased to see her. Mum gave them all lots of hugs and kisses. But Mum wasn't alone!

Hopscotch has been specially designed to fit the requirements of the National Literacy Strategy. It offers real books by top authors and illustrators for children developing their reading skills.

There are 25 Hopscotch stories to choose from:

Marvin, the Blue Pig
Written by Karen Wallace
Illustrated by Lisa Williams

Plip and Plop
Written by Penny Dolan
Illustrated by Lisa Smith

The Queen's Dragon
Written by Anne Cassidy
Illustrated by Gwyneth Williamson

Flora McQuack
Written by Penny Dolan
Illustrated by Kay Widdowson

Willie the Whale
Written by Joy Oades
Illustrated by Barbara Vagnozzi

Naughty Nancy
Written by Anne Cassidy
Illustrated by Desideria Guicciardini

Run!
Written by Sue Ferraby
Illustrated by Fabiano Fiorin

The Playground Snake
Written by Brian Moses
Illustrated by David Mostyn

"Sausages!"
Written by Anne Adeney
Illustrated by Roger Fereday

The Truth about Hansel and Gretel
Written by Karina Law
Illustrated by Elke Counsell

Pippin's Big Jump
Written by Hilary Robinson
Illustrated by Sarah Warburton

Whose Birthday Is It?
Written by Sherryl Clark
Illustrated by Jan Smith

The Princess and the Frog
Written by Margaret Nash
Illustrated by Martin Remphry

Flynn Flies High
Written by Hilary Robinson
Illustrated by Tim Archbold

Clever Cat
Written by Karen Wallace
Illustrated by Anni Axworthy

Moo!
Written by Penny Dolan
Illustrated by Melanie Sharp

Izzie's Idea
Written by Jillian Powell
Illustrated by Leonie Shearing

Roly-poly Rice Ball
Written by Penny Dolan
Illustrated by Diana Mayo

I Can't Stand It!
Written by Anne Adeney
Illustrated by Mike Phillips

Cockerel's Big Egg
Written by Damian Harvey
Illustrated by François Hall

The Truth about those Billy Goats
Written by Karina Law
Illustrated by Graham Philpot

Bear in Town
Written by A. H. Benjamin
Illustrated by Richard Watson

Marlowe's Mum and the Tree House
Written by Karina Law
Illustrated by Ross Collins

The Best Den Ever
Written by Anne Cassidy
Illustrated by Deborah Allwright

How to Teach a Dragon Manners
Written by Hilary Robinson
Illustrated by Jane Abbott